·JULIUS·
THE BABY OF THE WORLD

BY KEVIN HENKES

SCHOLASTIC INC.

New York Toronto London Auckland Sydney
Mexico City New Delhi Hong Kong

ISBN 0-590-10896-4

Copyright © 1990 by Kevin Henkes.
All rights reserved. Published by Scholastic Inc., 555 Broadway,
New York, NY 10012, by arrangement with Greenwillow Books,
a division of William Morrow & Company, Inc.
SCHOLASTIC and associated logos are trademarks and/or registered
trademarks of Scholastic Inc.

26 25 24 23   5 6 7 8/0

Printed in the U.S.A.   40

Watercolor paints and a black pen were used for the full-color art.
The text type is Cochin.

· FOR SUSAN ·

THE EDITOR OF THE WORLD

Before Julius was born, Lilly was the best
big sister in the world.
She gave him things.
She told him secrets.
And she sang lullabies to him every night.

After Julius was born, it was a different story.
Lilly took her things back.
She pinched his tail.
And she yelled insulting comments into his crib.

"I am the queen," said Lilly. "And I hate Julius."

But her parents loved him.
They kissed his wet pink nose.
They admired his small black eyes.
And they stroked his sweet white fur.

Lilly thought his wet pink nose was slimy.
She thought his small black eyes were beady.
And she thought his sweet white fur was not so sweet.
Especially when he needed his diaper changed.
"Julius is the baby of the world," chimed Lilly's parents.
"Disgusting," said Lilly.

Lilly had to share her room with Julius.

"After Julius goes away, do I get my room
back?" she asked.

"Julius isn't going anywhere," said Lilly's mother.
And he didn't.

He stayed and stayed and stayed.

Lilly was supposed to be very quiet while Julius slept.
"After Julius goes away, can I talk like a normal person
  again?" she shouted.
"Julius isn't going anywhere," said Lilly's father.
And he didn't.
He stayed and stayed and stayed.

"We want Julius to grow up to be as extraordinary as you,"
said Lilly's mother, "so we must tell him constantly how
beautiful he is and how much we love him."
When no one was looking, Lilly had her own idea.

"We want Julius to grow up to be as clever as you," said
Lilly's father, "so we must sing him his numbers and letters
whenever possible."

When no one was looking, Lilly had her own idea.

Lilly's parents were more than a bit doubtful about
leaving the two of them alone together.
Lilly tried to frighten Julius with her nifty disguises.
She learned magic and tried to make him disappear.
When that didn't work, she simply pretended that he
didn't exist.

Lilly spent more time than usual in the uncooperative chair.

Lilly's parents showered her with hugs and kisses
and treats of all shapes and sizes.
They even let her stay up fifteen minutes later every night.
It didn't matter. Nothing worked.

"I am the queen," said Lilly. "And I hate Julius."

But her parents loved him.
They kissed his wet pink nose.
They admired his small black eyes.
And they stroked his sweet white fur.

"Julius is the baby of the world," chimed Lilly's parents.
"Disgusting," said Lilly.

Lilly's parents were amused when Julius blew a bubble.
"Can you believe it?!" they exclaimed.
  But if Lilly did the exact same thing, they said,
"Lilly, let's mind our manners, please."

Lilly's parents were dazzled when Julius babbled and gurgled.
"Such a vocabulary!" they exclaimed.
  But if Lilly did the exact same thing, they said,
"Lilly, let's act our age, please."

Lilly's parents were amazed when Julius screamed.
"What lung capacity!" they exclaimed.
But if Lilly did the exact same thing, they said,
"Lilly, let's restrain ourselves, please."

One morning, while Lilly was busy playing opera,
her mother said, "Why don't you put some of that verbal
exuberance to good use? Why don't you tell Julius
a nice story?"
"He's too little to understand a story," said Lilly.
"He can understand it in his own way," said Lilly's mother.
"Okay," said Lilly, smiling.

"JULIUS, THE GERM OF THE WORLD.

BY ME," said Lilly.

"Once upon a time," said Lilly, "there was a baby.

His name was Julius.

Julius was really a germ.

Julius was like dust under your bed.

If he was a number, he would be zero.

If he was a food, he would be a raisin.

Zero is nothing.

A raisin tastes like dirt.

The End," said Lilly.

The story earned her ten minutes in the uncooperative chair.

Lilly warned her friends Chester and Wilson and Victor about babies. "Trust me, they're dreadful," she said.

She warned strangers about babies, too.
"You will live to regret that bump under your dress," she said.

Lilly ran away seven times in one morning.
"I'm *really* leaving this time," she called.
"Who knows where they'll find me."

The same afternoon Lilly had a tea party and everyone came.
Everyone but Julius.
"His invitation must have been lost in the mail," she explained.

Lilly had glorious dreams about Julius.

And ghastly nightmares, too.

Lilly's parents showered her with compliments and praise
and niceties of all shapes and sizes.
They even let her drink her juice out of the antique china cup.
It didn't matter. Nothing worked.

"I am the queen," said Lilly. "And I hate Julius."

But her parents loved him.
They kissed his wet pink nose.
They admired his small black eyes.
And they stroked his sweet white fur.

"Julius is the baby of the world," chimed Lilly's parents.
"Disgusting," said Lilly.

When Lilly's mother felt up to it, she planned
a festive celebration in honor of Julius.
All the relatives came. There was quite a spread.
"What's the big deal?" said Lilly. "Haven't they
all seen a silly lump before?"

Apparently not. All afternoon the relatives hovered
over Julius.
They kissed his wet pink nose.
They admired his small black eyes.
And they stroked his sweet white fur.

"Disgusting," said Cousin Garland.

"What?" said Lilly.

"Julius," said Cousin Garland. "I think his wet pink nose
is slimy. I think his small black eyes are beady.
And I think his sweet white fur is not so sweet.
He needs his diaper changed."

Lilly's nose twitched.
Her eyes narrowed.
Her fur stood on end.
And her tail quivered.

"You're talking about my brother," said Lilly.
"And for your information, his nose is shiny,
his eyes are sparkly, and his fur smells like perfume."

Cousin Garland was speechless.

"He can blow bubbles," continued Lilly. "He can babble
and gurgle. And he can scream better than anyone."

Cousin Garland tried to slink out of the room.

"Stop!" said Lilly. "I am the queen. Watch me closely."

Lilly picked up Julius.
She kissed his wet pink nose.
She admired his small black eyes.
And she stroked his sweet white fur.

"Your turn," said Lilly, handing Julius over to Cousin Garland.
"Kiss! Admire! Stroke!" Lilly commanded.

"Now repeat after me," said Lilly. "Julius is the
baby of the world."
"Julius is the baby of the world," said Cousin Garland.
"Louder!" said Lilly.
"JULIUS IS THE BABY OF THE WORLD!"

And from then on, he was. In everyone's opinion.
Especially in Lilly's.